MADELINE AND THE BAD HAT

Also by Ludwig Bemelmans

MADELINE
AND THE BAD HAT

WRITTEN AND ILLUSTRATED BY

Ludwig Bemelmans

SCHOLASTIC

Originally published in the USA in 1956 as a limited autographed
edition by The Viking Press, Inc
First trade edition published in the USA in 1957 by The Viking
Press, Inc
First published in the UK in 1958 by Andre Deutsch Ltd
This edition first published in 1996 by Scholastic Children's Books
Euston House, 24 Eversholt Street
London NW1 1DB
a division of Scholastic Ltd
www.scholastic.co.uk
London ~ New York ~ Toronto ~ Sydney ~ Auckland
Mexico City ~ New Delhi ~ Hong Kong

ISBN 978 1407 11054 7

1 3 5 7 9 10 8 6 4 2

MADELINE AND THE BAD HAT

To
Mimi

In an old house in Paris
That was covered with vines
Lived twelve little girls
In two straight lines.
They left the house at half-past nine
In two straight lines, in rain or shine.
The smallest one was MADELINE.

One day the Spanish Ambassador

Moved into the house next door.

Look, my darlings, what bliss, what joy!

His Excellency has a boy.

Madeline said, "It is evident that
This little boy is a Bad Hat!"

In the spring when birdies sing
Something suddenly went "zing!"

Causing pain and shocked surprise
During morning exercise.

On hot summer nights he ghosted;

In the autumn wind he boasted

That he flew the highest kite.

Year in, year out, he was polite.

He was sure and quick on ice,

And Miss Clavel said, "Isn't he nice!"

One day he climbed upon the wall
And cried, "Come, I invite you all!
Come over some time, and I'll let you see
My toys and my menagerie—
My frogs and birds and bugs and bats,
Squirrels, hedgehogs and two cats.
The hunting in this neighbourhood
Is exceptionally good."

But Madeline said, "Please don't molest us,
Your menagerie does not interest us."

He changed his clothes and said, "I bet
This invitation they'll accept."

Madeline answered, "A Torero
Is not at all our idea of a hero!"
The poor lad left; he was lonesome and blue;
He shut himself in—what else could he do?

But in a short while, the little elf
Was back again, and his old self.

Said Miss Clavel, "It seems to me
He needs an outlet for his energy.

"A chest of tools might be attractive
For a little boy that's very active.

"I knew it—listen to him play,
Hammering, sawing, and working away."

Oh, but that boy was really mean!

He built himself a GUILLOTINE!

He was unmoved by the last look
The frightened chickens gave the cook.

He ate them ROASTED, GRILLED and FRITO!
Oh, what a horror was PEPITO!

One day, when out to take the air,

Madeline said, "Oh, look who's there!"

Pepito carried a bulging sack.

He was followed by an increasing pack

Of all the dogs in the neighbourhood.

"That boy is simply misunderstood.

Look at him bringing those doggies food!"

He said, "Let's have a game of tag—"
And let a CAT out of the bag!

There were no trees, and so instead
The cat jumped on Pepito's head.

And now just listen to the poor
Boy crying, "AU SECOURS!"
Which you must cry, if by any chance
You're ever in need of help in France.

Miss Clavel ran fast and faster
To the scene of the disaster.

She came in time to save the Bad Hat,
And Madeline took care of the cat.
Goodbye, Fido; so long, Rover.
Let's go home—the fun is over.

There was sorrowing and pain

In the Embassy of Spain.

The Ambassadress wept tears of joy,
As she thanked Miss Clavel for saving her boy.

"Nothing," said the Ambassador,
"Would cheer up poor Pepito more
Than a visit from next door.

"Only one visitor at a time,
Will you go in first, Miss Madeline?"

So Madeline went in on tiptoe,
And whispered, "Can you hear me, Pepito?
It serves you right, you horrid brat,
For what you did to that poor cat."

"I'll never hurt another cat,"
Pepito said. "I swear to that.
I've learned my lesson. Please believe
I'm turning over a new leaf."
"That's fine," she said. "I hope you do.
We all will keep our eyes on you!"

And lo and behold, the former Barbarian

Turned into a Vegetarian.

And the starling and turtle, the bunny and bat,

Went back to their native habitat.

His love of animals was such,

Even Miss Clavel said,

"It's too much!"

The little girls all cried "Boo-hoo!"

But Madeline said, "I know what to do."

And Madeline told Pepito that
He was no longer a BAD HAT.
She said, "You are our pride and joy,
You are the world's most wonderful boy!"

They went home and broke their bread
And brushed their teeth and went to bed,

And as Miss Clavel turned out the light
She said, "I knew it would all come out right."